THE REALMS OF LIGHT AND SHADOW:

Part 1: MEGALOMANIA

This work is entirely fictional and not based on true stories—or is it? Any resemblance to real people, places, or events is purely coincidental... and if you notice any uncanny parallels, just blame the pen!

The Realms of Light and Shadow:
Part 1: Megalomania

First edition. July 28, 2024.

Written by: Mina Mikhaeil.

Index

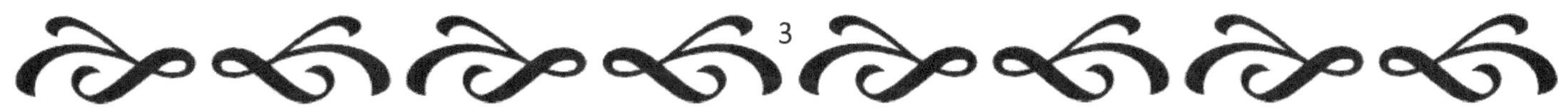

Characters

King Alden: The just and wise king of Elaria.

Queen Elara: King Alden's wife.

Prince Alaric: Alden's heir, brave and noble.

Princess Yara: Alden's daughter, intelligent and graceful.

Prince Edwin: Alden's youngest son, young yet wise.

Sir Percival: Alden's wise minister.

Lady Thalia: Queen Elara's maid and spy.

Lord Fares: Queen Elara's personal guard.

King Luther: The power-hungry king of Draven.

Queen Morgana: Luther's deceitful wife.

Prince Cedric: Luther's heir, gentle and peace-loving.

Princess Seraphina: Luther's daughter, a kind-hearted princess.

Princess Isabella: Luther's youngest daughter, compassionate and intelligent.

Sir Reginald: Luther's cunning and ambitious minister.

Lysander: The wandering bard who tells revealing stories in rhyming poetry.

Prologue

Within the heart of a vast kingdom in the far lands, where the shadows of castles loom over villages and the clatter of swords echoes through the dense forests, two distinct realms stand in stark contrast.

The Kingdom of Elaria, under the just and wise rule of King Alden, gleams as a beacon of fairness and wisdom. King Alden's reign is marked by his unwavering commitment to justice and the well-being of his people. He is known for his fair and impartial judgments, ensuring that every citizen, regardless of their status, receives equal treatment under the law. His wisdom is evident in the well-thought-out policies and reforms he has implemented, which have led to a flourishing economy and a peaceful society.

The Kingdom of Draven, ruled by the ruthless and ambitious King Luther, whose reign is marked by unrelenting ambition and cruelty. The king's relentless ambition drives him to seek expansion and dominance at any cost. This ambition fuels a series of aggressive military campaigns aimed at expanding Draven's borders, leading to frequent conflicts with neighboring kingdoms.

Their intertwined fates weave a compelling tale of bravery, deep love, and shifting alliances, each kingdom's destiny forever linked in a story of epic proportions.

Chapter 1

The
Just King
&
His Realm

    King Alden of Elaria was a beacon of hope and justice. His realm flourished under his benevolent rule, with thriving farms, happy subjects, and a palace filled with wisdom and love. His unmatched compassion extended beyond his court; he personally ensured the well-being of the less fortunate and always offered a listening ear to his people. His wise judgments were never swayed by personal gain, earning him the respect and loyalty of all. Beside him was his wise minister, Sir Percival, whose counsel was invaluable.

    Sir Percival acquired his knowledge and wisdom through years of dedicated study and experience in various lands, learning from scholars and sages. His reputation grew as he resolved complex disputes and offered invaluable advice to both royalty and commoners alike. His fame spread across the realms through tales of his fair judgments and strategic insights, establishing him as a revered figure in the art of governance and diplomacy.

Queen Elara, Alden's wife, is beautiful and seemingly kind. Her face is a portrait of grace, with delicate features that speak of both strength and softness. Her eyes, a captivating shade of emerald green, hold a spark of warmth and intelligence, though they can quickly turn cold and calculating. Her smile, radiant and enchanting, has the power to light up a room, yet it often conceals the machinations of a shrewd mind. Her hair flows like a river of gold, cascading in perfect waves down her back, complementing her flawless, porcelain-like skin that seems to glow in the softest light. Her figure is elegant and statuesque, a testament to both poise and allure. Yet behind her facade lie hypocrisy and deceit.

Princess Yara, Alden's daughter, is a symbol of grace and intelligence. She has a heart as pure as her father's and a mind as sharp as Sir Percival's. Her presence exudes a natural elegance that captivates everyone she meets, while her insightful perspectives on matters of state demonstrate a maturity beyond her years.

Prince Alaric, the heir, is a brave and noble young man, deeply in love with the people and his kingdom. His unwavering dedication to justice and his genuine concern for his subjects are evident in every decision he makes.

In this era of prosperity, the kingdom of Elaria experienced remarkable growth and development. New wells were dug throughout the land, ensuring that even the most remote villages had access to clean water. The fertile soil was being cultivated more efficiently, with expansive fields of crops sprouting across the kingdom. Innovative farming techniques were introduced, leading to a bountiful harvest that fed not only Elaria but also its neighboring lands.

The construction of grand new castles and charming houses dotted the expanding landscape, creating vibrant communities and enhancing the kingdom's defensive capabilities. These architectural marvels stood as symbols of Elaria's strength and progress, welcoming new settlers and fostering a sense of security and stability.

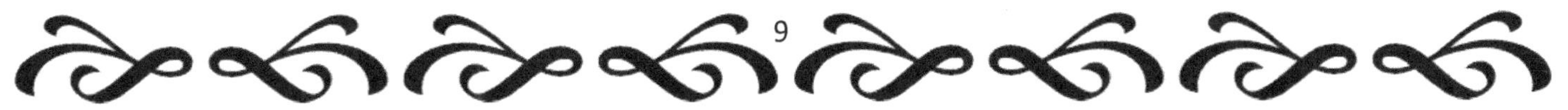

King Alden's diplomacy flourished as he established valuable alliances with neighboring realms, strengthening both political and economic ties. Under his guidance, Elaria engaged in prosperous trade agreements. These alliances not only bolstered the kingdom's wealth but also paved the way for cultural exchange and mutual support, with his castle serving as a beacon of wisdom and peace. In stark contrast, King Luther of Draven ruled with an iron fist, instilling fear among his people. His castle, shrouded in secrecy, was a center of dark clandestine operations, highlighting the stark differences between the two kingdoms.

Chapter 2

Shadows over The Dark Kingdom

King Luther of Draven ruled with an iron fist, his intelligence shadowed by his malevolence. Though smart and cunning, he was a tyrant whose subjects lived in constant fear, his court rife with intrigue and treachery. His minister, Sir Reginald, was equally shrewd and knowledgeable, known for his wisdom and depth of understanding. However, Reginald's thirst for power was insatiable, and he did not shy away from using underhanded methods to achieve his goals.

Queen Morgana, Luther's wife, was the epitome of deceptive beauty. Her intelligence matched her husband's, but her cunning was cloaked in a veneer of grace and allure. Morgana's beauty was enchanting: her face, a perfect oval with high cheekbones, was framed by cascades of raven-black hair that shimmered like silk. Her eyes, a piercing emerald green, seemed to see into the souls of those around her, her smile both captivating and dangerous. Her figure was both elegant and seductive, commanding attention and desire.

Princess Seraphina, Luther's daughter, is a breathtaking beauty whose kindness shines through a demeanor shaped by her parents' cold expectations. Her grace and charm surpass even Queen Morgana's, captivating all who meet her. With eyes like pure sapphires and a smile that warms the coldest hearts, Seraphina embodies genuine warmth and empathy.

Despite her parents' cunning and ambition, Seraphina is an outgoing and kind-hearted soul. Though she may lack their sharp intellect, her pure love and compassion endear her to all. She is cherished by the people for her decency and dedication to their well-being, often found among villages, tending to the poor and offering support. Seraphina's respect for everyone, regardless of status, makes her a beloved figure whose beauty radiates from within, truly embodying the spirit of a people's princess.

In the depths of Draven Kingdom, beneath the facade of royal splendor, a web of malevolent schemes and clandestine operations unfurls. King Luther's rule, though outwardly authoritative, is marred by a sinister agenda crafted in the shadows. His court, a breeding ground for deceit, hides the true extent of his ambitions. Here, plans are meticulously laid out to expand his dominion through a network of espionage and covert manipulation.

Sir Reginald, ever the schemer, orchestrates a series of covert operations designed to destabilize neighboring realms. Reginald's ambition knows no bounds; he envisions an empire forged through treachery and subterfuge, using his extensive knowledge to exploit every vulnerability in his adversaries' defenses.

Queen Morgana, with her beguiling beauty and treacherous mind, is the mastermind behind the kingdom's most insidious plots. Her charm masks a cruel strategy of psychological warfare, aimed at weakening the resolve of opposing rulers. She deploys her network of informants to spread misinformation, manipulate public sentiment, and create conflicts that serve her husband's ambitions. Morgana's ability to sway opinions and influence decisions through her allure only strengthens Draven's position.

In the shadows of the palace, and secret meetings take place, where occult practices and forbidden magic is employed to secure the kingdom's dominance. These arcane endeavors are aimed at enhancing their power and ensuring their control over every aspect of their subjects' lives. The king and queen, surrounded by their most trusted and malevolent advisors, plot the downfall of their enemies with cold, calculated precision.

Despite the darkness enveloping the kingdom, a glimmer of hope shines through. Princess Seraphina, along with her sister, Princess Isabella, have received an invitation from Princess Yara of Elaria. This gesture of goodwill signifies a burgeoning friendship between the two royal families, hinting at the possibility of a peaceful alliance and mutual support. As the Dark Kingdom continues its shadowy pursuits, the bond between Seraphina and Yara grows stronger.

Chapter 3

Bonds
Of
Heirship

Prince Cedric of Draven, the heir to King Luther, is a gentle soul caught between his father's ruthless expectations and his own desire for peace. He is a valiant knight, renowned for his strength and skill in battles, leading his father's army with unwavering bravery and strategic brilliance.

Despite the ferocity he exhibits on the battlefield, Cedric is known for his kindness and respect towards both his allies and foes. His merciful nature and profound courage have earned him the admiration and loyalty of his troops, while his wisdom and fairness make him a beloved figure among the people.

Cedric's heart yearns for peace, and his actions reflect a noble pursuit of justice and compassion, making him a Shining Example in a kingdom overshadowed by his father's tyranny.

Despite their fathers' enmity, Alaric and Cedric forge a secret friendship, meeting in hidden glades and abandoned ruins. Their bond, strengthened by heartfelt correspondence and clandestine meetings, becomes a source of solace and hope amid ongoing conflict.

They exchange letters filled with hopes and strategies for peace, actively collaborating on initiatives to foster goodwill between their lands.

Cedric supports Alaric's aspirations for justice, while Alaric appreciates Cedric's bravery and honor. Their shared vision for a united future—built on love and justice—illuminates a path toward reconciliation, signaling that even in discord, a new era of unity may emerge.

Chapter 4

The Minister's Masterstroke

Sir Percival, always alert to the growing unrest in Elaria's court, devised a plan to expose Queen Elara's hidden deceit, suspecting that beneath her polished exterior lay a web of lies and manipulation. To uncover the truth, he enlisted the help of Lysander, a mysterious wandering bard renowned for blending truth with fiction in his tales.

Elara's secret plans are both subtle and dangerous. She secretly forms alliances with King Luther to undermine Elaria and increase her power, with the ultimate goal of marrying him to rule both kingdoms. Their scheme involves getting rid of Alden and Morgana, whom they plan to kill to secure their path to power. Her secret assistant is Lady Thalia, a skilled spy with connections to the darker side of the realm. Their plot includes tampering with trade deals, secretly supporting rebels within the kingdom, and orchestrating the deaths of Alden and Morgana.

Percival's plan relies on Lysander's special skills. Known for his talent in blending into any society and uncovering secrets through his performances, Lysander agrees to help expose Elara. He travels across the kingdom, collecting evidence and spreading rumors that will eventually lead to her downfall.

Lysander has traveled through thirteen kingdoms, gaining knowledge about court politics and intrigue.His extensive network of contacts, built over years of travel, provides him with valuable insights into the schemes of powerful people.

To get into King Alden's palace, Lysander uses his poetry skills to win over the court. He is invited as a performer at a grand feast hosted by Alden. His performance cleverly highlights the difference between truth and deceit, captivating the court and earning the trust of key figures, including Sir Percival. Posing as a celebrated artist, Lysander moves freely through the palace, gathering important evidence and watching Elara's secret activities.

Lysander's role is crucial; his ability to gather information and subtly influence opinions helps Percival expose Elara's treachery. As the evidence against Elara builds up, Percival prepares to reveal her deceit to the court, using Lysander's findings to dismantle her network of lies and restore integrity to Elaria's rule.

With everything set and the pieces falling into place, Sir Percival and Lysander work tirelessly to ensure that the truth comes out, protecting the kingdom from Elara's hidden schemes and bringing justice back to the realm.

Chapter 5

Lysander's Tales

Lysander arrived at the Elarian court entrance; his presence humble but his words powerful. He spoke in simple, rhyming poetry, captivating the court with stories that held hidden truths. King Alden, intrigued, welcomed him warmly.

Lysander made his grand entrance into the Elarian court with an air of understated elegance. As he walked in, he began reciting a poem with a rhythmic grace, his voice rising and falling with the cadence of his words.

Beneath the moon's gentle light,

Truth and lies prepare to fight.

A queen's heart may seem so pure,

Yet hidden motives none endure.

Queen Elara felt a chill as Lysander's words struck close to home.

The court was instantly captivated by his performance; their eyes followed him in awe as he wove tales with his verses. As the final lines of his poem lingered in the air, a profound silence enveloped the room, each listener absorbing the weight of his message.

The queen, Queen Elara, could not hide the unease that crept over her. She suspected that Lysander's poem, with its subtle hints and poignant truths, might be aimed at uncovering the secrets she worked so hard to conceal. Her eyes narrowed slightly as she watched him, a flicker of suspicion in her gaze.

King Alden, intrigued by the bard's earlier work, encouraged Lysander to continue.

"Please, proceed with another of your tales," he said, eager to hear more.

With a graceful bow, Lysander began a new poem, one designed to charm and uplift. His words celebrated the beauty of the kingdom and the virtues of its rulers. Each verse flows with elegance, capturing the essence of the realm's splendor and the nobility of its leaders. The poem's rhythm and imagery resonate with heartfelt admiration, reflecting Lysander's deep respect for the land and its sovereigns.

"In this realm where roses bloom,

The king's kindness banishes gloom.

The queen's grace, a radiant light,

Guides our land through day and night.

A kingdom blessed with such delight,

Its people prosper in a shining light."

Lysander glided gracefully across the grand hall, his flowing robes swirling with each step.

His hands wove intricate patterns in the air, punctuating the rhythm of his verses, while his footfalls matched the melody. As he moved, he continued to recite his poems, his voice rising and falling in harmony with his performance, creating a captivating display that mesmerized everyone present.

His dance and poetry intertwined seamlessly, making each verse come alive with the grace of his movements and the beauty of his words.

"From the mountains high to valleys deep,

Where rivers dance and willows weep,

The songs of joy and laughter ring,

Echoes of peace that our hearts sing.

In every corner, every street,

Harmony and love so sweet.

The queen's smile, like dawn's first gleam,

Washes over the land like a dream.

And with the king's unwavering might,

We stand together, strong and right.

In this realm of vibrant cheer,

We cherish moments year by year.

With every dawn and twilight's grace,

Our kingdom thrives in its warm embrace."

…

"Our kingdom thrives … in its warm embrace."

The court responded warmly to this new piece, their earlier tension easing as Lysander's poetic praise filled the room. Even Queen Elara, though still cautious, felt a touch of comfort from the bard's flattering words. The atmosphere lightened, and Lysander's performance, while subtle in its praise, helped to soothe the queen's growing discomfort.

As Lysander concluded his mesmerizing performance, the room erupted in applause, and King Alden, visibly impressed, extended his gratitude with a warm smile. *"Your poetry has truly enchanted us,"* the king said. *"Please, join us at the royal table; we would be honored to share a meal and converse with you."*

Lysander graciously accepted the invitation, and as he took his place among the nobles, the conversation flowed effortlessly, with the king and court eagerly discussing the bard's travels and the inspiration behind his captivating verses.

Chapter 6

Unraveling The Dark Deceit

As the days passed, the situation became more intense. Sir Percival and Lysander gathered enough proof to reveal Queen Elara's hidden plots, and Lysander's tales grew more direct, exposing her treachery. They presented their findings to King Alden, whose shock quickly turned into action. Guided by Sir Percival, Alden confronted his wife in front of the stunned court. Elara's facade crumbled under the weight of the revelations, leading to her immediate departure and the exposure of her deceit.

King Alden acted with profound wisdom in the wake of the revelations. Despite the gravity of Queen Elara's treachery, he decreed that no harsh action be taken against her. Instead, he called for a grand ceremony to address the matter. In his address, Alden acknowledged that everyone is fallible and that mistakes, while regrettable, are part of the human condition. He emphasized the importance of mercy and understanding, underscoring that the strength of the kingdom lies in its unity. The ceremony was a poignant reminder of the values that hold the realm together. The king's words were heartfelt and sincere, reinforcing the commitment to maintain harmony and compassion despite the turmoil. The people, moved by his leadership, reaffirmed their loyalty to their sovereign and the principles of their beloved kingdom.

After the ceremony, Queen Elara, deeply unsettled by the turn of events, immediately summoned Lord Fares. In the privacy of her chambers, she anxiously recounted the day's revelations and the unexpected leniency of King Alden. She confided her concerns about Lysander and his potential threat to her remaining influence. Elara instructed Fares to investigate Lysander thoroughly, to uncover any hidden motives or secrets the bard might possess. She demanded a comprehensive report on Lysander's background, his true intentions, and any connections that could be leveraged against him. With her empire at stake, Elara's determination to secure her power drove her to act swiftly and decisively.

Lysander, aware of the growing threat from Queen Elara and her attempts to undermine him, recognized that staying in Elaria could jeopardize his safety. Fearing for his well-being, he decided it was best to leave Elaria. With his mind set on ensuring his protection, Lysander prepared to continue his journey. He set his sights on the neighboring Draven kingdom, hoping to find refuge and perhaps even new opportunities for his talents. As he departed, he carried with him the knowledge that his presence in Draven could hold new possibilities, both for himself and for his ongoing mission.

Chapter 7

Intrigue Within the Shadowed Court

Meanwhile, in Draven, King Luther was growing wary of Lysander's influence. When Lysander arrived in Draven, Luther dismissed him with little interest in his poetry, preferring instead the entertainment of female dancers and sword combats. However, Luther was keen to gather any intelligence about Elaria. The following day, he invited Lysander to dine with him, lavishly providing wine in the hope of making the bard somewhat inebriated before questioning him. As the wine took effect, Lysander's guard dropped, and he inadvertently revealed key details about Queen Elara's schemes being exposed.

Though Lysander was given a modest room to rest and restricted to performing only at smaller gatherings, he still managed to attract a considerable audience with his captivating presence.

As Lysander prepares for an intimate gathering, he pens a new song, "A Song of Mistakes and Hope," to express his reflections on human error and the enduring power of hope. The song is born from his recent regret after realizing that, in his drunken state, he had inadvertently let slip some critical information about Elaria. His melodies, now tinged with a sense of remorse, aim to soothe and inspire, resonating with the essence of learning from one's mistakes and finding renewal.

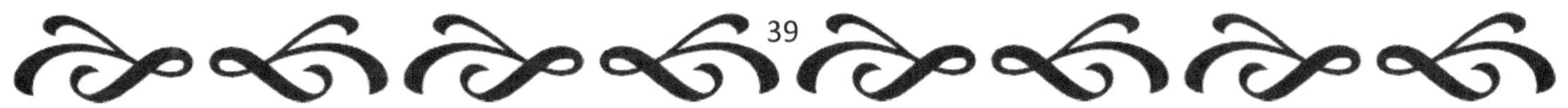

In life's grand dance, mistakes we make,

Through missteps, hearts and dreams may break.

Regret may follow close behind,

Yet hope persists in troubled mind.

Though shadows cast their fleeting spell,

Our inner light can break the shell.

From every choice, both wrong and right,

We learn to mend and seek the light.

For every path we wander through,

We have the chance to start anew.

Embrace the flaws, the trials faced,

And find the strength to be embraced.

So let us strive through darkened plight,

With hopeful hearts and spirits bright.

For though mistakes may mark our way,

The dawn of hope will bring a new day.

Chapter **8**

Veiled Hearts and Silent Longing

In the verdant expanses lying between the two kingdoms, a realm of breathtaking beauty unfolds. Amidst the rolling fields, lush gardens bloom with vibrant flowers, their colors vivid against the backdrop of majestic trees. The air is filled with a fresh, invigorating breeze that dances over crystal-clear lakes, creating a serene and enchanting atmosphere. Here, in this tranquil haven, Alaric and Seraphina find solace from their busy lives.

They often meet in these secluded gardens, away from the prying eyes of their courts. Alaric, with his noble bearing and thoughtful eyes, speaks with quiet resolve, while Seraphina, graceful and radiant, listens with concern. On this occasion, they sit by the edge of a shimmering lake, their conversation turning to the shadows of their respective kingdoms.

Alaric shares his unease about the growing tensions in Elaria, voicing his worries over Lysander's revelations and the shifting dynamics within his own realm. Seraphina, equally troubled, reveals her own kingdom's internal strife and the unsettling secrets she has learned about her mother. As they confide in each other, their hearts are heavy with the weight of their kingdoms' secrets, yet their bond grows stronger, united by their shared fears and hopes for a better future.

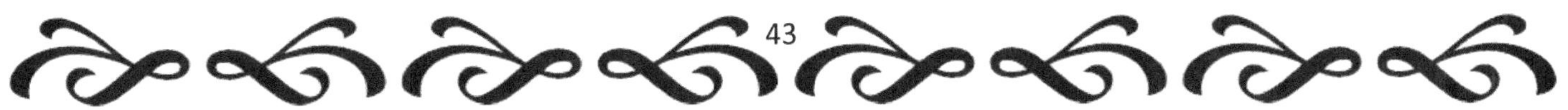

Alaric notices the shadow of worry dimming their once magical moments together. The weight of their kingdoms' troubles has cast a pall over their secret rendezvous. Determined to rekindle the enchantment of their meetings, he rises from their secluded bench by the serene pond.

The air is crisp and filled with the sweet scent of blooming flowers. Alaric gestures towards a vibrant rose bush, its petals a burst of color against the tranquil waters. The roses, rich in hue and full of life, stand in stark contrast to the muted tones of their current mood. "Look at this beautiful rose bush," he says softly, hoping to draw her gaze away from the swirling storm of their responsibilities.

He gently takes Seraphina's hand, his touch warm and reassuring. With a tender smile, he leads her towards the rose bush. The soft rustling of leaves and the gentle ripple of the pond create a peaceful backdrop as he wraps his arm around her waist. They begin to sway in a slow, intimate dance, the world around them fading into a blur of soft colors and soothing sounds.

As they move together, Alaric's voice, smooth and heartfelt, begins to weave a romantic poem:

"Through night and day, my heart shall stay,

Bound to yours in love's sweet sway.

No walls or crowns can keep apart,

The love that binds our beating heart.

In gardens bright where roses grow,

Our dreams take flight, our futures show.

With every step and every glance,

We weave a tale of timeless romance.

As stars above our love will shine,

And guide us through this life's design.

Together we shall face the storm,

In love's embrace, we find our form.

Let future days be filled with cheer,

Our hearts entwined, forever near.

In fields of hope, our love will bloom,

Casting light and chasing gloom."

  Alaric's voice trails off as the last notes of his poem hang in the air, mingling with the fragrant scent of roses and the gentle lapping of the pond. The dance draws them closer, momentarily shielding them from the harsh realities of their world.

Seraphina gazes up at him with eyes that shimmer with emotion. Her heart races as the romantic words and the intimacy of the dance envelop her in a cocoon of warmth and affection. She feels a mixture of joy and vulnerability, her cheeks flushed with a soft pink hue. The serenity of the moment, coupled with Alaric's heartfelt poem, stirs a deep sense of connection within her. Seraphina leans in closer, her head resting gently against Alaric's shoulder as she breathes in the sweet scent of roses. Her heart swells with love and hope, and she allows herself to savor this fleeting escape from the outside world. The weight of their shared romance feels like a promise of brighter days ahead, and she silently cherishes the tender moment they share, feeling truly seen and cherished for the first time.

Chapter 9

Schemes Of the Council

In the heart of Draven, Lysander, the wandering bard, had become more than just a guest; he was a well-informed confidant to a group of insiders. These allies, intrigued by Lysander's tales and seemingly unassuming nature, had confided in him about the kingdom's hidden dynamics. Through whispered conversations in dimly lit chambers, Lysander learned unsettling news. Rumors were circulating that King Luther had sinister plans to consolidate power. The king was reportedly gathering all available troops, preparing for a large-scale invasion of Elaria. The goal was to seize control of both kingdoms, extending his dominion beyond Draven's borders. This information painted a grim picture of impending conflict, with Luther's ambitions threatening to plunge both lands into chaos.

Amidst these revelations, Sir Reginald, an influential figure within Draven's court, was plotting his own ambitious scheme. Reginald had secretly aligned himself with various powerful allies within the army, all of whom were discontented with Luther's rule. Their shared dissatisfaction fueled a plan to assassinate Luther and his queen during the anticipated war. Reginald's ultimate aim was to seize control of both kingdoms, positioning himself as the new ruler. His plans included a dark strategy to force Isabella, a key figure in his scheme, into marriage, solidifying his claim to the throne. Reginald's calculated moves and widespread support within the army set the stage for a fierce power struggle.

In the midst of these swirling plots, Lysander found himself in the company of Prince Cedric and his sisters. The royal siblings welcomed him with genuine warmth, eager to hear his counsel. Lysander, recognizing the significance of the moment, shared his insights on leadership and governance. He spoke of the importance of wisdom, compassion, and strategic thinking. Cedric and his sisters, attentive and respectful, were pleased to hear that their reputations preceded them in a positive light. The conversation was filled with mutual respect and curiosity as they sought advice from the seasoned traveler.

Among the royal siblings, Isabella, known for her grace and intelligence, engaged Lysander in a heartfelt conversation. She asked him to share a poem, sensing that his words carried the wisdom and inspiration they needed. Lysander, with a warm smile, obliged. Rising from his seat, he began to recite a poem that spoke to the core of good and evil, kindness and justice. Each verse was dedicated to the individuals present, highlighting their virtues and tender hearts:

"In lands of shadows, light will shine,

Through Isabella's heart so kind.

With grace and wisdom, strong and fair,

She weaves a future beyond compare.

Prince Cedric, brave with courage bold,

In his actions, a story told.

For justice, honor, he stands tall,

Guiding his people through rise and fall.

To the future king, I humbly say,

Your reign will guide a brighter day.

May your kingdom finds the peace it seeks,

As hope and love your future speaks.

Good deeds and hearts so true,

Will bring the light, as dawn's anew.

In unity, may thee find thy might,

A prosperous realm in purest light."

The poem resonated deeply with everyone present, filling the room with a sense of joy and hope. Their smiles and nods of appreciation reflected the impact of Lysander's words.

Later, Lysander had a private moment with Prince Cedric. He shared his concerns about the impending conflict and offered a cautious warning. Based on his analysis and the information he had gathered, Lysander predicted that supporting his father's aggressive stance would lead to defeat. He suggested that Cedric use his influence to persuade the king to reconsider the war strategy. Instead, Lysander proposed forging alliances and initiating trade to ensure stability and prosperity for both kingdoms.

Cedric, valuing the wisdom in Lysander's advice, expressed his gratitude. The prince was moved by the bard's insights and promised to consider his recommendations carefully.

Chapter 10

Children's Wisdom Unveiled

Prince Cedric, sensing the importance of a private discussion, sent a discreet message to Prince Alaric. He conveyed that it was time for them to talk about pressing political matters of their kingdoms, suggesting a meeting in private. Shortly after, Cedric receives Alaric's warm reply, accepting the invitation and suggesting a meeting in Elaria.

Cedric prepared for the journey, bringing his sisters along for the trip. As they traveled, their guards became concerned when they noticed a figure trailing them. The mysterious person approached and revealed himself as a messenger from King Luther. The messenger warned Cedric and his party of potential danger and urged them to return to Draven immediately for their safety.

Despite the warning, Cedric and his sisters chose to continue their journey to Elaria. They assured the messenger that they were well-guarded and asked him to return to King Luther with their regards and reassurance.

Meanwhile, in Draven, Lysander continued his quest to gather information and draw closer to the king. His aim was to subtly influence King Luther against initiating a war with Elaria. However, the king remains focused on war preparations, ensuring the army is fully equipped and ready for the impending conflict.

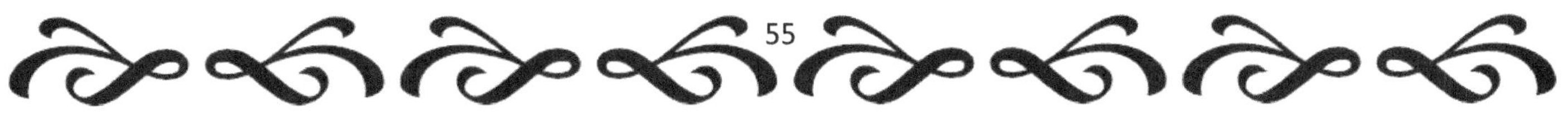

Prince Cedric and his sisters arrived in Elaria to a warm and grand welcome. The royal entourage greeted them with enthusiasm and escorted them to their luxurious rooms, allowing them time to rest and refresh after their journey.

Later that evening, a small party was held in their honor, where Cedric and his sisters were treated to a delightful evening of dancing, dining, and laughter. The guests enjoyed an array of delicious foods and engaging conversations, creating a festive atmosphere that made everyone feel at ease.

As the night drew to a close, Cedric and his sisters retired to their rooms, content and ready for rest. They looked forward to their important meeting the following morning, knowing that it would be a pivotal moment in their diplomatic visit.

Early the next morning, they awoke to the pleasant sound of bells ringing through the city. At first, they wondered if it was an emergency or a warning, but the melodious and comforting tone of the bells eased their worries. The sound was soothing, not alarming, and they enjoyed it as they dressed and made their way to the meeting room for their first diplomatic encounter.

As they headed to the meeting room, they were met halfway by Prince Edwin, who greeted them warmly and explained the tradition. "The bells are rung each morning as part of one of our cherished traditions. It's meant to start the day on a positive note and help everyone wake up at the same time, beginning their day with a smile. It also fosters a sense of unity and order among our people."

Prince Edwin continued, sharing more about Elaria's traditions as they walked. "We also have a tradition of communal meals where everyone gathers, and our festivals are designed to bring people together and celebrate our shared values."

When they arrived at the meeting room, Prince Alaric and Princess Yara were already present. They began the meeting with a lavish meal, enjoying fine dishes and engaging in light conversation. The room was filled with pleasant chatter, but soon a moment of silence settled over them as everyone wondered who would start the serious discussions.

Princess Isabela took the initiative to break the silence: *"My father, King Luther, is preparing the army, and I find his decisions increasingly difficult to support. They seem harsh, and I worry about the impact on our people."*

With a calm yet firm expression, Edwin responded: *"Father's decisions, though harsh, are often for the greater good."*

Isabela's brow furrowed in distress as she countered his viewpoint: *"But at what cost? Our people suffer. Can we not find a path of compassion?"*

Prince Alaric, with a thoughtful look, interjected diplomatically: *"Isabela raises a valid point. We must consider the welfare of our people and seek a solution that minimizes suffering."*

Cedric, earnest and reflective, spoke pragmatically: *"It is clear that both our kingdoms face significant challenges. Perhaps a different approach could help us avoid unnecessary conflict."*

Princess Yara, intrigued, turned to Cedric for insight: *"What kind of approach do you have in mind, Cedric?"*

Cedric responded inclusively, outlining a path forward: *"A dialogue between our kingdoms might reveal common ground and prevent further escalation. We should explore peaceful negotiations before resorting to war."*

Edwin, nodding, voiced his support for a peaceful resolution: *"Peaceful negotiations are best. We must understand each other's perspectives and work towards mutual benefits."*

Isabella, encouraged by the consensus, voiced her agreement: *"I agree. We should strive for a solution that respects the needs and concerns of both sides."*

Alaric, resolute, ended the discussion on a hopeful note: *"Let's focus on a diplomatic resolution. This meeting should build trust and explore agreements."*

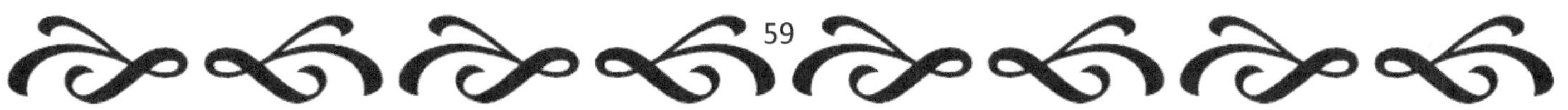

Cedric, smiling at the united front, expressed his optimism for the future: *"I'm glad we agree. Let's work together for a prosperous future for both our kingdoms."*

Yara, her eyes bright with hope, endorsed the collaborative spirit: *"Indeed. If we can unite our efforts, we will be better equipped to face any challenges that arise."*

Edwin, optimistic, offered a final note of encouragement: *"Let us move forward with a spirit of cooperation. This meeting is a promising step towards a peaceful and prosperous relationship."*

~~~

The conversation continued with hope and a shared commitment to finding a peaceful resolution. Despite its simplicity, the dialogue hinted at future leaders who will seek a balance between justice and mercy. The positive atmosphere set the stage for future discussions and collaboration between the two kingdoms, reflecting their mutual desire for a harmonious and just future.

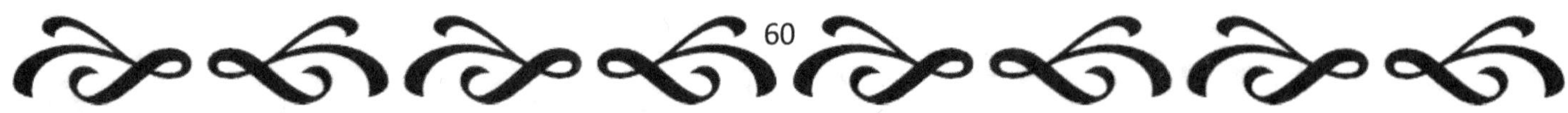
~~~

Chapter 11

Clash For the Crown

King Luther's army began its march towards Elaria with determined precision, causing a ripple of panic and urgency throughout the land. In a desperate bid to alert Elaria, Lysander made the arduous journey with all haste, arriving breathless and exhausted. His arrival was met with concern as he quickly briefed Prince Alaric and Prince Cedric about King Luther's aggressive move. His news prompted immediate action: King Alden was swiftly informed and ordered his forces to prepare for battle. A messenger was dispatched to King Luther to seek clarification on his intentions.

The atmosphere in the palace grew tense as the heirs, Alaric and Cedric, exchanged worried glances, feeling helpless and uncertain about the impending conflict. Their discussions were cut short when King Alden summoned them. The king, with a reassuring presence, promised their safety despite the looming threat of war.

In the midst of this turmoil, Lysander's spirits were deeply affected. His heart ached at the thought of how fleeting peace could be and how frequently wars disrupted the calm. To express his sorrow and apprehension, he began to sing a mournful poem, his voice tinged with sadness:

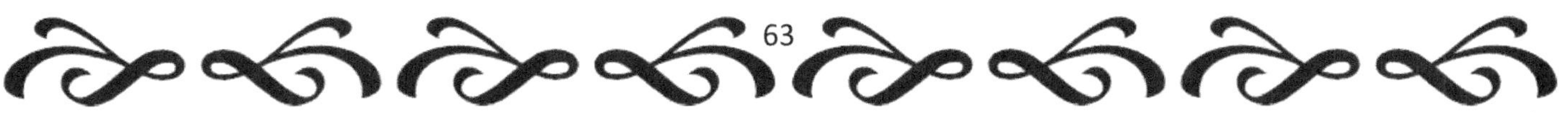

In peaceful days we long to stay,

Yet war comes swiftly, peace gives way.

With heavy hearts, we face the fight,

For fleeting peace, we yearn each night.

The calm we crave is lost so soon,

In wars we find our harshest boon.

In peaceful days we long to stay,

Yet war comes swiftly, peace gives way.

"Peace gives way ... peace gives way"

Tensions escalated as Luther is marching towards Elaria. Right before the kingdoms clashed in a fierce battle, Prince Alaric, Prince Cedric, and Prince Edwin took a bold step to intervene.

Each rushed between the two armies, desperate to avert the looming conflict and advocate for peace.

Prince Alaric approached King Luther, his demeanor calm but urgent. "King Luther, please reconsider this course of action. We stand on the brink of unnecessary bloodshed. There must be another way to resolve our differences."

King Luther, his face set in grim determination, responded coldly. "*The time for negotiation has passed, Alaric. Elaria's refusal to yield has left me no choice but to proceed with my plans. The only acceptable outcome now is the immediate surrender of your kingdom.*"

Prince Alaric tried to offer an alternative, his voice firm yet pleading. "*I am prepared to meet any of your demands to preserve peace. We can discuss terms that allow both kingdoms to remain independent while addressing your concerns. Let us find a solution that avoids further suffering.*"

King Luther's eyes narrowed. "*My terms are non-negotiable. Surrender Elaria now, or face the consequences.*"

Despite Prince Alaric's earnest attempt to negotiate, the situation rapidly deteriorated.

Without warning, King Luther signaled his forces, and the army surged forward, plunging into battle. The clash was immediate and fierce, with swords clashing and the roar of combat filling the air.

Prince Cedric, seeing the inevitable escalation, urged Prince Alaric to retreat. "Alaric, we must pull back from the front lines. Our priority now should be to safeguard our sisters and plan for the aftermath of this conflict. We need to think strategically."

Reluctantly, Prince Alaric agreed, and the both hurried to their sisters' side. They gathered in a safe location in Elaria, away from the chaos of battle.

Princess Isabela spoke with concern. "What should we do now? The war is upon us, and we need to prepare for both immediate safety and the future."

Princess Seraphina, her face a mask of worry, added, "We need to ensure that our people are protected and that we have a plan for the days following the battle. Should we consider any diplomatic options or alliances?"

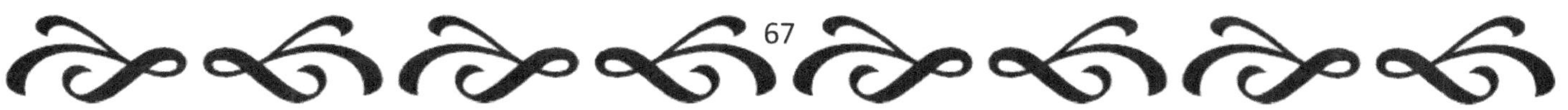

Prince Cedric nodded; his expression thoughtful. "We should focus on maintaining the safety of our kingdoms and our people. Once the immediate threat is dealt with, we can explore diplomatic channels to negotiate a lasting peace."

Prince Alaric, though weary, was resolute. "Agreed. Let's regroup and plan our next steps carefully. We will need to stay united and vigilant. Our kingdom's future depends on how we handle this crisis and the aftermath of the conflict."

The siblings, though anxious, felt a renewed sense of purpose as they prepared for the challenges ahead, determined to navigate the complex web of war and diplomacy with wisdom and courage.

They remained calm and devised a plan to disperse themselves, along with the remaining guards, to direct all the people of Elaria to safe places away from the war zone. Their strategic efforts aimed to ensure the safety of their citizens amidst the chaos, reflecting their commitment to both leadership and the well-being of their people.

By nightfall, the battle had concluded, and the outcome was clear: King Luther lay defeated, having met his end on the battlefield. Sir Reginald, too, had fallen beside him, their ambitions extinguished in the chaos of war. King Alden, gravely wounded, had been forced to retreat to his palace, his strength diminished but his spirit unbroken.

Lysander, witnessing the aftermath of the conflict, felt a deep sadness and frustration over the decisions that had led to such devastation. As he roamed the battlefield, his anger was intense, and he expressed his feelings through a heartfelt verse:

> *"Bravery lies in hearts so true,*
>
> *But greed and power, they undo.*
>
> *A king's strength is in his heart,*
>
> *Not in tearing worlds apart."*

Determined to aid the wounded, Lysander moved among the injured soldiers, offering assistance. Yara, Seraphina, and Isabella joined him, their faces showing concern. Together, they treated wounds, provided comfort, and transported the injured to Elaria for proper care.

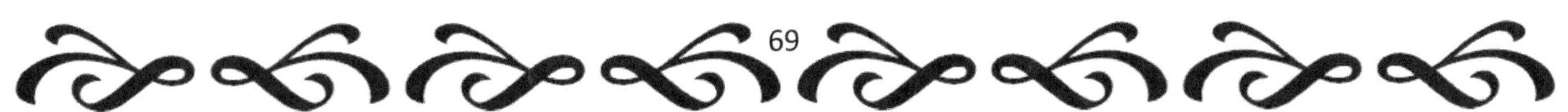

As they worked, the sight of lifeless bodies filled them with profound sorrow. Moved by the tragedy, Lysander sang a mournful poem about the battle's toll on both sides.

In fields where valor once held sway,
Now lies the blood of those who'd stay.
In battles fought by might and pride,
Many a soul in shadows died.

Helpless we stand against the tide,
When kings with greed and power stride.
They command, we obey in vain,
And peace slips by, a fleeting train.

Yet hope remains, a guiding light,
Through darkest days and longest night.
We must keep faith, let hearts embrace,
The promise of a peaceful place.

Peace is our hope, our hearts' true guide,
Peace is our hope, where dreams abide.

As Lysander's voice faded into the night, the somber reflection of the battle's impact lingered. Despite the grief, the hope for a future marked by peace shone through, guiding their efforts to heal and rebuild in the aftermath of the conflict.

As Princess Isabella tirelessly tended to each wounded soldier she could find, exhaustion began to take its toll. Despite her fatigue, she persisted, driven by a sense of duty and compassion. The soft, mournful strains of Lysander's singing seemed to provide her with a renewed strength. She clung to the final lines of his song, repeating them to herself:

> Peace is our hope, our hearts' true guide,
>
> Peace is our hope, where dreams abide.

She whispered these words over and over, even as her energy waned. Her resolve lasted until she nearly fainted from extreme exhaustion. With the darkness settling in and the battleground becoming perilous, their guards set up tents for shelter. The group spent the night on the field, surrounded by the remnants of the battle.

At dawn, they returned to Elaria after aiding many soldiers from both sides. They continued daily to nurse the wounded back to health. A week later, Cedric's concern for his mother and kingdom grew. He wondered, "How is Mother? What has happened to our kingdom? Are the people managing? Could someone be plotting for the throne? Will order be restored, or has chaos prevailed?"

After a moment of deep contemplation, Cedric turned to his sisters and said, "We need to leave immediately. I must return to Draven."

Seraphina and Isabella exchanged worried glances. Isabella voiced her concern, "What awaits us back home? After emerging from war, what more could be in store?"

Cedric's swift departure left everyone anxious and unsettled as he exchanged hasty farewells and prepared to return to his kingdom.

He senses the worry weighing on his sisters' hearts. To comfort them and lift their spirits, he decides to sing a fast-paced song. His goal is to entertain them during the trip, dispel their fears, and restore their strength. As his lively tune fills the air, Cedric's energetic voice and catchy melody aim to replace their anxiety with hope and encouragement.

Here comes a prince, brave and bold,

Through lands of silver and of gold.

With every trial, with every strife,

His sisters' strength brings him to life.

> **Across the seas and through the dark,**
>
> **Their bond ignites his fiery spark.**
>
> **Barriers rise, yet he stands tall,**
>
> **With his sisters' strength, he conquers all.**

Here comes a prince, brave and bold,

Through lands of silver and of gold.

With every trial, with every strife,

His sisters' strength brings him to life.

> **Their love and courage are his guide,**
>
> **Through every challenge, by his side.**
>
> **The prince faces fears and shadows deep,**
>
> **But with his sisters, victory he'll keep.**

Here comes a prince, brave and bold,

Through lands of silver and of gold.

With every trial, with every strife,

His sisters' strength brings him to life.

Upon hearing Cedric's upbeat song, the guards felt inspired to participate. Their voices, strong and supportive, blended harmoniously with Cedric's as they sang along. The infectious rhythm of the song quickly filled the air, transforming the mood from one of anxiety to one of camaraderie and joy.

The melody of "Here comes a prince" resonated through the countryside, each line sung with enthusiasm. The guards' voices added depth and warmth to the tune, their collective effort aimed at bringing a smile to the faces of the weary princesses.

As the sun dipped lower in the sky, casting a warm, golden hue over the landscape, the guards decided to add their own spin on the song. They sang it together, their voices rising and falling in harmony, infusing the melody with new, cheerful verses.

The fresh words they introduced were not only delightful but also added a special touch to the performance, making the song even more enjoyable, lifting everyone's spirits and creating a pleasant atmosphere on their journey.

Through every trial, through every test,
He will overcome and will be the best,
With two loyal sisters!

In the darkest night or the brightest day,
He'll conquer troubles, he'll find his way,
With two loyal sisters!

Foes and dangers are no match,
He always wins every match,
With two loyal sisters!

Every challenge, every fight,
He'll triumph with them by his side,
With two loyal sisters!

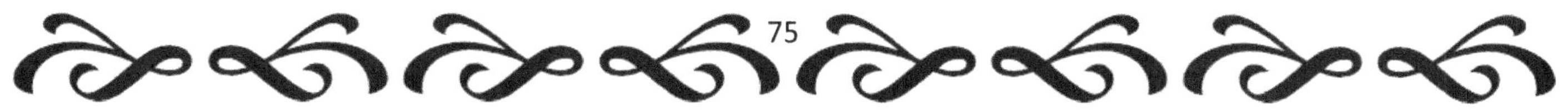

The princesses, initially surprised, found themselves comforted by the heartfelt gesture. Their worried expressions softened, replaced by smiles as they joined in the singing.

The journey, though still fraught with uncertainty, became a bit lighter, thanks to the shared effort of the prince and his loyal guards. The song's uplifting rhythm helped dissipate their fears, if only for a moment, and gave them the strength to face whatever lay ahead with renewed hope and unity.

As the sun began to set, casting long shadows over the landscape, the group arrived at the imposing gates of Draven. The sight that greeted them was unexpected. The usually bustling gates stood eerily silent, with no guards in sight. The faces of the few townsfolk milling about were downcast and somber, adding to the air of foreboding.

Moments after their arrival, Lysander appeared, accompanied by forty guards from Elaria, sent by Prince Alaric to offer assistance and support. As the people began to recognize Prince Cedric and his sisters, a flicker of joy spread through the crowd. They gathered around the royal family, greeted them with smiles and welcomed them back.

However, the brief sense of relief was shattered when two of the royal guards, tasked with protecting Queen Morgana, approached Prince Cedric with grim expressions. Their voices were heavy with sorrow as they delivered the devastating news: Sir Reginald had orchestrated a plot to assassinate the queen during the king's absence. Tragically, the queen was now dead.

The news hit Princess Isabela and Princess Seraphina like a tidal wave. Their cries of anguish pierced the silence as they raced towards the palace, their hearts heavy with grief. Arriving at the palace, they found their mother's lifeless body placed on a makeshift altar, surrounded by a somberly prepared coffin. The sight of their beloved mother in such a state was unbearable.

The guards informed Prince Cedric of further troubling developments. Two other counselors, who had allied themselves with Sir Reginald, had fled Draven with around a hundred soldiers. They were now fugitives, adding another layer of turmoil to an already dire situation.

With a heavy heart, Prince Cedric swiftly assembled the remaining soldiers and issued orders for the funerals of the queen and king, ensuring their final rites were handled with the respect and dignity they deserved.

At the funeral, Morgana's heartfelt tribute came in the form of a poignant poem, a farewell to her parents. Her voice trembled as she recited the lines, each word a reflection of her deep sorrow:

In my heart, your love will stay,

Guiding me through every day.

Memories of your warm embrace,

Forever etched, time can't erase.

Though you're gone, your spirits shine,

Your love remains, forever mine.

With tears streaming down her face, Morgana repeatedly uttered the final line of the poem, her voice breaking with each repetition:

"Your love remains, forever mine."

"Your love remains, forever mine."

The funeral was a somber affair, marked by the deep mourning of the royal family and the people of Draven. The loss of their queen and the turmoil that lay ahead cast a long shadow over their hearts.

Chapter 12

Love
Amidst
The Ashes

The war ended with Luther's defeat, but the victory was tinged with sorrow. News of King Alden's death, resulting from severe wounds in battle, spread quickly.

The people of Draven, uneasy about the outcome, feared that King Alaric, the new ruler, might seek revenge for the aggression against Elaria.

Sensing the growing unrest, King Cedric was determined to restore peace and stability. He convened his counselors to strategize and seek their advice.

Meanwhile, Alaric, feeling a deep longing for Seraphina, set up a private meeting in their secluded lakeside garden - the serene spot where they could be free from unwanted attention.

Alaric: "*Seraphina, these past days have shown me how precious our moments together are. I miss you dearly and wish to make our bond permanent.*"

Seraphina: "*I've missed you as well, Alaric. This time apart has only made me more certain of my feelings.*"

Alaric: "*I am overjoyed to hear that. I'll speak to your brother about our plans and ensure everything is arranged for our union. We'll make sure our families are united and our lands find peace once more.*"

Seraphina and Alaric were both overwhelmed with excitement at the thought of their future together. They felt a deep connection and shared a vision of a life filled with love and unity. Seraphina, feeling the emotions of the moment, decided to express her feelings through song.

She began to sing a heartfelt ballad, her voice filled with warmth and passion. The song, with its enchanting melody, spoke of their dreams and the joy of being together forever. The lyrics were a beautiful testament to their love and the promise of a shared future.

Upon the dawn of love, my heart was bound,

A flame ignited by your tender gaze.

In dreams, your voice is all that I have found,

A melody that fills my silent days.

Your eyes, like stars, lead through the night so clear,

Their light a beacon guiding me to thee.

Though lands may part us, love will always adhere,

In their glow, our hearts are ever free.

Yet time's cruel hand doth stretch lands apart,
And still, my yearning grows with every breath.
For you are the true compass of my heart,
Without you, all joy gives way to death.

The distance fades when dreams of you appear,
In whispered moments when we're far apart.
Our souls entwined, our bond is crystal clear,
No force can sever what's held in the heart.

Though shadows loom and trials may come near,
Our love's resilience will not ever cease.
In every storm, through every doubt and fear,
We find our haven in our sweet release.

So let the world spin on, for we shall be
Together still, in love's eternity.

When shadows fall and light fades away,
In love's embrace, together we shall stay.

Chapter 13

A New Dawn: Renewed Harmony

  A few weeks had passed. King Cedric sent a messenger to King Alaric with an important request. Cedric wished to arrange a visit to Elaria, as he had a significant proposal to discuss.

King Alaric responded with enthusiasm, welcoming Cedric back to Elaria. In his reply, Alaric extended the invitation not only to Cedric but also requested that he bring the princesses and his trusted advisors or counselors. The meeting was anticipated to be pivotal, and Alaric wanted all the key figures present to ensure a thorough and fruitful discussion.

King Cedric and King Alaric had meticulously planned their crucial meeting, a rendezvous set to take place in the grandest ballroom of Elaria's palace. This was no ordinary meeting; it was one that could either usher in a new era of eternal peace or potentially drive a wedge between their kingdoms. The anticipation was palpable, and the stakes could not have been higher. Both monarchs knew the weight of their decisions would resonate far beyond this single day.

As the day of the meeting arrived, the grand ballroom was a sight to behold. The opulent decor, lavish food, and flowing drinks created an atmosphere of grandeur and anticipation. King Alaric welcomed King Cedric with all the splendor befitting such an important occasion, and the two leaders settled into their seats amidst the splendor of the ballroom.

The conversation began in high spirits, but soon the tone shifted as King Cedric initiated the serious discussion he had been contemplating for months. With the future of both kingdoms hanging in the balance, he outlined his plan for restoring peace. Cedric's proposal was both bold and sincere: an end to the hostilities and the beginning of a new era marked by unity and cooperation. He believed this was the best path to ensure that no more wars would scar their lands.

Then, with unwavering resolve, King Cedric stood and made a momentous announcement: he was formally proposing to marry Princess Yara. The room fell into a profound silence, the weight of Cedric's words hanging heavily in the air.

King Alaric, initially taken aback by the unexpected proposal, maintained a serious demeanor as he processed the revelation. The silence stretched on, filled with unspoken questions and mounting tension. Everyone present —princesses, counselors, and guests—could sense the gravity of the situation. If Alaric were to reject the proposal, the repercussions could be dire. Draven's fear might escalate, and the fragile friendship between the kingdoms could crumble.

The atmosphere grew thick with suspense as the silence continued. Just as hope seemed to wane, King Alaric finally broke the stillness with a small, enigmatic smile. He addressed King Cedric with a single condition for his acceptance of the proposal: Cedric must first agree to Alaric's own request.

A wave of surprise rippled through the room. The room buzzed with whispers as people speculated on the implications of this new proposal, and what the condition might entail. Was it a demand for a significant portion of Cedric's lands, a hefty sum of gold, or something even more unexpected? The anticipation was palpable as everyone wondered if Cedric would agree.

King Cedric, though initially taken aback, quickly regained his composure. With a warm smile, he expressed his willingness to accept the condition, highlighting the bond of friendship that had always existed between him and Alaric. He eagerly asked what the condition was.

King Alaric took a few deliberate steps toward King Cedric, his expression softening into a warm smile. With a tone both confident and gentle, he declared that before he could approve Cedric's proposal, Cedric must first agree to a condition of his own. The condition was that Cedric must also consent to Alaric's desire to marry Princess Seraphina.

The room fell into a stunned silence as the gravity of Alaric's request settled over everyone. The guests had anticipated demands for lands or treasures, but the proposal was unexpectedly personal. Now, it seemed that the union of the kingdoms hinged on both kings agreeing to marry the sisters of each other. The atmosphere buzzed with speculation—would Cedric agree to Alaric's condition?

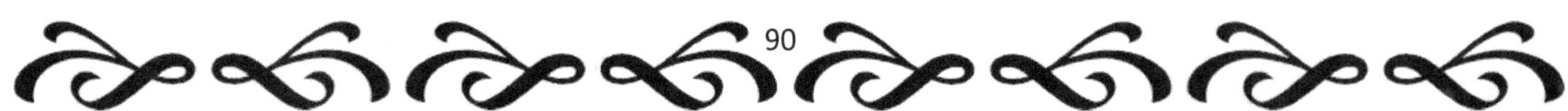

King Cedric's face slowly broke into a smile as the realization of Alaric's condition dawned on him. Though initially taken aback, he felt a surge of happiness inside. His mind raced with thoughts of the future—of joyous weddings and grand celebrations in both kingdoms. He envisioned a time of lasting peace and prosperity, where the people of both realms would live in harmony. The thought of a united future, filled with shared joy and tranquility, brought a sense of fulfillment that made it difficult for him to speak immediately. The dream of a new era of peace and happiness was within reach, and Cedric could hardly contain his excitement.

The room was filled with a collective gasp of surprise as the true nature of the condition became clear. The request was personal and heartfelt—each king seeking to marry the sister of the other. The tension that had pervaded the room now transformed into eager anticipation.

As both kings stood close, looking each other in the eye, the atmosphere was charged with expectation. The two monarchs shook hands, their grip firm and respectful, symbolizing their commitment to the newfound alliance.

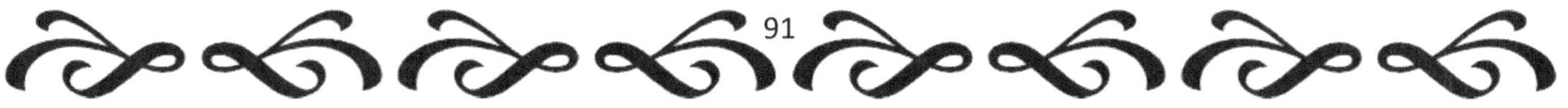

With the handshake, a wave of relief and joy washed over everyone present. Cheers erupted throughout the ballroom, and the sound of jubilation filled the air. The guests, their faces alight with happiness, began to envision the bright future of peace and celebration that awaited both kingdoms. The prospect of joyous weddings and harmonious celebrations filled their hearts, heralding a new era of unity and prosperity.

As the celebratory mood took hold, both kingdoms sprang into action, swiftly arranging the wedding ceremonies for the two royal couples. The grand halls of Elaria and Draven became abuzz with activity, as flowers were arranged, invitations were sent, and the finest garments were prepared. It was a time of jubilant preparation and high anticipation.

King Cedric was overjoyed. The weight of his responsibilities seemed lighter as he envisioned a future filled with love and unity. With every detail of the wedding being meticulously planned, Cedric felt a profound sense of relief and happiness. The prospect of marrying Princess Yara brought him immense joy, and he found himself daydreaming about a peaceful future where their children would grow up in a world free from conflict. His heart swelled with pride and hope as he imagined the beautiful life they would build together.

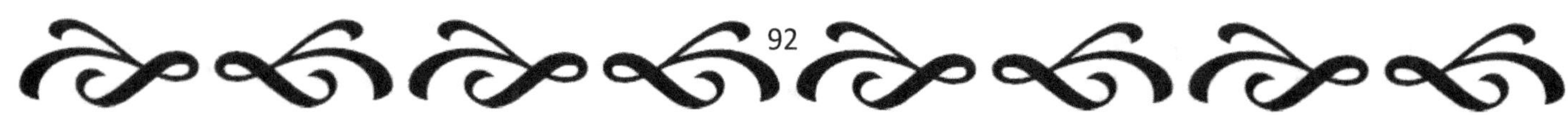

Princess Yara, radiant with excitement, eagerly prepared for her new life as Queen. She delighted in the prospect of marrying Cedric, whom she had come to cherish deeply. The preparations for the wedding filled her with a sense of purpose and joy. Yara found solace in the fact that this union symbolized the end of a turbulent era and the beginning of a harmonious future. Her heart fluttered with anticipation, and she eagerly looked forward to their life together.

King Alaric, felt a deep sense of contentment as the wedding plans progressed. The proposal from Cedric, which he had greeted, now seemed like a perfect resolution. Alaric's thoughts were consumed with the joy of marrying Princess Seraphina. His heart was warmed by the thought of a united kingdom and the end of hostilities. The sense of camaraderie and the promise of a peaceful future made him smile with genuine satisfaction.

Princess Seraphina was overwhelmed with happiness. The delightful proposal from Alaric filled her with a profound sense of joy. She eagerly anticipated the start of their shared life, filled with dreams of unity and peace. Her heart leaped at the thought of marrying the prince she had long admired and respected. The prospect of becoming queen and contributing to the prosperity of both kingdoms excited her immensely.

Prince Edwin also felt a profound sense of relief and joy as the wedding preparations unfolded. The harmony between the kingdoms meant that the diplomatic efforts had borne fruit, and he could now look forward to a future where his family would be united with another royal line. Edwin's heart was full of pride as he witnessed the culmination of effort and struggle. The upcoming celebrations were not just a personal joy but a symbol of enduring peace, which both kings had worked so hard to achieve.

Princess Isabella, though concerned about the past, found solace in the new era of peace. The weddings brought her a sense of relief and hope for a better future. She felt a deep sense of satisfaction seeing her brother's happiness and the unity between the kingdoms. Isabella was excited about the upcoming celebrations, which symbolized not just personal joy but also a hopeful new chapter for both realms. The thought of peace finally settling over their lands filled her with a renewed sense of optimism.

For nearly nine months, peace and harmony reigned between the two kingdoms, bringing renewed unity. However, troubling news soon disrupted the tranquility, spreading sorrow and uncertainty from Elaira to Draven. This unsettling news threatened to overshadow the promising future of both realms, casting a veil of unease over the previously celebratory atmosphere.

Chapter 14

A Spark Kindles a New Tale

As the kingdoms of Elaria and Draven basked in the glow of their newfound harmony, a shadow fell over King Aleric and Queen Seraphina of Elaria as they grappled with profound sorrow. Seraphina had suffered a heartbreaking loss, having lost her baby during childbirth. Despite the joyful celebrations surrounding the births, this loss weighed heavily on their hearts.

In contrast, Queen Yara of Elaria had delivered a healthy and thriving baby, bringing a beacon of happiness to both her and King Cedric. Though Seraphina was deeply saddened by her personal tragedy, she found solace in the joy of her brother and his wife. Her happiness for their family was tinged with the pain of her own loss, creating a complex tapestry of emotions as she navigated this bittersweet chapter in her life.

While the kingdoms celebrated the marriages and the birth of new life, Seraphina's grief was a poignant reminder of the fragility of joy amidst the intertwining threads of sorrow and celebration.

Conclusion

As this chapter's curtain starts to cling,

We promise a new tale where destinies swing,

"The Enduring legacy of the just king",

where new adventures and echoes will ring.

~ ~ ~

The upcoming chapters promise to unveil a tapestry of mysteries and challenges, blending magic with conspiracy. Expect a dark shadow and the emergence of a new light that will push both kingdoms to their limits. Stay tuned to discover what lies ahead in this ever-evolving tale.

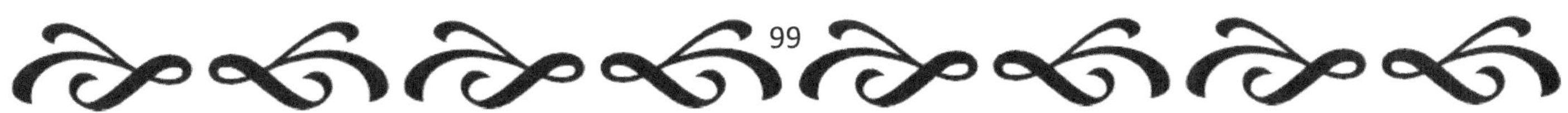